FANTASTICAL MOMENTS

A FANTASY SHORT STORY COLLECTION

ERUDESSA GENTIAN

ERUDESSA GENTIAN

CONTENTS

1. The Wolfe Pack's Chosen   1

2. Alive   6

3. Why Me?   10

4. Monsters Made   15

5. What's in a Gift?   23

6. Crashed Plans   32

About The Author   42

THE WOLFE PACK'S CHOSEN

WAR OF WOLVES AND DRAGONS

Athalulf, proud heir to the powerful Blood Wolfe Pack, was trapped.

He realized, belatedly, why his kind were forbidden from visiting the human world before coming of age. Until he grew into his powers, Athalulf was practically no different than any regular wolf in England. He was going to be in so much trouble when his father discovered his absence.

Hours of slogging through marshes had dyed his rust-colored fur a muddy brown. His small body had grown tired and sore, his paw pads torn from struggling along rough terrain.

He'd slipped out of the Wolfe Domain, near the Wulfsige estate, hadn't he? Or had he miscalculated?

At the founding of England, the Dragons had granted their blessing to the first King, Athelstan Drake, and his family. They declared that a single Chosen from each generation would be gifted with enhanced speed, strength, and the magical Dragon's Breath.

In turn, the Wolves decided to pick their own Chosen from the bloodline of the king's best friend and most powerful supporter, the Honorable Duke James Wulfsige.

But Wolves and Dragons are notoriously hard to please. So whilst the Dragons' gifts were inherited from generation to generation, the Wolves could, and often did, go hundreds of years before acknowledging a Chosen.

Ever since he was a pup, Athalulf dreamed of finding the next Chosen. He had snuck into England today hoping to observe the current Wulfsige members. Surely they had produced a worthy candidate or two over the last thousand years.

But right now, his body was weary from traveling. Catching a whiff of something delicious, Athalulf followed his nose to a hanging deer carcass. Humans could wait. Right now, he was hungry.

Athalulf gathered his haunches underneath him and gave a powerful leap. His razor teeth clamped down on the raw flesh. But as soon as his weight started to drag the deer's body down, Athalulf heard a hiss from above.

Startled, he let go of the deer, falling straight into a large metal contraption. With a final blast of steam, the cogwheel mechanism locked into place.

Suppressing a frightened howl, Athalulf strained against the thick sides. Fruitless. A whine of anxiety escaped as he desperately clawed at the bars.

A young female voice interrupted his efforts. "Vincent, you know papa doesn't like you trapping animals."

"Uncle doesn't appreciate my progressive genius. Those old-fashioned hunts he loves so much are doomed in the wake of steam-powered inventions!"

The haughty young boy stomped through the trees, closely followed by a plump little girl. Both children froze when they caught sight of the snarling Athalulf.

The girl had a thick headful of curly red hair, and her green eyes held both shock and worry. Her lacy brown dress spoke of nobility.

Vincent's fine tweed suit was covered in broken branches and leaves. Hiis brown hair glinted with auburn highlights.

"I caught a wolf!?" Vincent crowed in delight. "Not even uncle will be able to deny me this!"

Vincent spun around and disappeared back into the trees, whooping and hollering.

The girl glanced nervously toward her departing cousin before swiftly moving toward the trap. Athalulf snarled louder and made a swipe for her pale arm.

"Please wait, Mr. Wolf." Her soft voice soothed his growling to a low rumble. "I'm trying to help, I promise. We are supposed to treasure wolves in this family, but my cousin merely wishes to use wolves as another stepping stone to more power. He won't take care of you. He will use you."

Her little fingers finally unlocked Athalulf's prison.

Athalulf sprang out of the trap, but was hesitant to leave the little girl. He liked her voice, and wanted to express his gratitude for her help. But the sound of twigs being broken underfoot made his hackles rise. The girl paled. Vincent was coming back.

"Go, run!" she begged.

Athalulf quickly nuzzled her cheek, then turned and ran soundlessly into the brush.

He soon collided with something the size of a horse.

Oh dear.

Athalulf crouched before his father in repentant submission.

Before the lecture could start, they heard angry voices, a sharp crack, then a cry of pain.

Athalulf tried to jump up, but his father's paw held him sprawled on the ground.

Father! She helped me! he pleaded.

It felt like an eternity passed before Athalulf's father picked him up by the scruff and bounded with him toward the voices. They crouched behind bushes to watch what was going on.

Vincent and two adult men stood around the crying little girl. She held her cheek while a trickle of blood ran from her lip.

Athalulf growled, but quieted when his father's paw landed on his back again.

Not yet, son. Strong amber eyes studied the humans. *They are Wulfsige.*

Athalulf's eyes widened with excitement. The girl could be their next Chosen!

"How dare you let Vincent's catch go, Ylva!" one of the men roared.

Ylva Wulfsige. Athalulf mulled the name in his head. *I like her, Father.*

Athalulf felt a rumble of approval.

"But uncle...papa!" Ylva stifled her sobs. "What if it was a Wolfe?"

"Then even more reason to keep it!" Vincent shook her. "They could have made me their Chosen!"

Anger rolled off of Athalulf as the group dragged Ylva off, still berating her. He struggled to go after them, but his father somberly shook his head.

You can't help her yet. Come home and call a Council. She will have to wait for the Pack.

Athalulf reluctantly followed his father further into the woods.

I

For more information about War of Wolves and Dragons, go to ErudessaGentian.com/writing

ALIVE

I was five the first time breathing felt like flames ripping my chest apart. Since then, mysterious illnesses cropped up, one by one. Pain lit up my right hip, while my left side periodically went numb. Eventually, I lost all feeling in my left foot. My spine fused together, making smooth movements nigh impossible, and I have lived with a constant roar in my head for the last five years. To top it off, I sometimes convulse helplessly, like I'm being possessed.

My parents and I have been to the most powerful—and expensive—Maedics on all three inhabited planets, but no one has been able to figure out what is truly wrong with me, much less why it happened or how to help me. They couldn't find any curses, no antidotes, no answers.

Maedics, coming from the high-class Forgor species, think themselves all-knowing and all-powerful. They hate cases like mine, because my existence proves them to be as fallible as any other race.

I hug my coat tightly around me, unable to control the intense pain spikes and the irritating buzz of my over-sensitized skin before being jostled around the crowded street again. I normally avoid people in general. Not only does my plethora of chronic illnesses make daily living a hellish chore, I also hate being labeled "The Diseased Girl."

It's not like I asked to spend the last twenty years in a fog of pain. And nothing I have is contagious, thank you very much.

I thought I had stopped expecting deliverance long ago, but apparently there's still an idiotic sliver of hope deep inside me. Why else would I have traveled hours to see this new Maedic everyone raves about?

Rumors talk about his healing power practically radiating off of him. If true, maybe just meeting him will bring me respite. Most Maedics can only help ten people before needing to rest, although I suspect part of that comes from their hatred of being touched. But reports claim this prodigy had cured an entire village in one sitting.

I sigh and shuffle into the long line of others waiting to see Maedic Aran. Maybe instead of being hopeful, I'm just desperate.

Perhaps, when this ends in another soul-crushing disappointment, I really will crawl off and let myself die —like I know everyone wishes I would do.

Judging from the talk swimming around me, Maedic Aran sounds unbelievable. I pray he actually sticks around long enough for me to approach him. Everybody knows Maedics are power hungry. But if you believe his fans, Maedic Aran truly seems to care more about the populace than lining his pockets.

I study the prodigious Maedic as I limp closer with the moving line.

He certainly appears like a typical Forgor Maedic, staying seated behind a small table. Nearly seven feet tall, ashen-gray skin, short blue hair. But good heavens, he's smiling at the people greeting him! I blink in surprise. Normally, Maedics view the regular populace with a cold disdain. In all my years of traveling from Maedic to Maedic, I don't think I've ever seen one smile before.

When my turn finally arrives, I lean against the table. My limbs ache from standing for so long. A town guard glares at me, but since my face clearly spells out the pain I'm in, they allow me to use the table for support.

"Hello." Maedic Aran smiles at me.

I'm taken aback at the warmth in his eyes, especially coming from a Maedic. Even other humans only scrutinize me with pity or disgust. I force my stiff facial muscles to smile back and try to answer his polite questions, but it's made difficult by my seldom-used, swollen throat.

"What is troubling you?" Maedic Aran asks kindly.

"What isn't?" My rough voice grates in my ears.

As we talk, I stealthily shift my right foot forward, my movements hidden by the table. Maybe he won't notice if I just tap his toe quickly. If a piece of his power can relieve even a smidgen of pain...Anything would be better than the agony I live with.

But even though I barely brush his foot, I know there is no hiding it from him.

His eyes widen as we both realize what I've done.

I'm frozen. Not only in fear, but in disbelief. Because the moment I touch him, my body becomes whole.

My spine straightens, the ache leaves my limbs, and feeling floods into my left side, which only adds to the dizzying sensation of all my torment flying away. I didn't know the absence of pain could make my breath stutter.

I don't understand what's happening. I can't even begin to decipher the whirlwind of emotions flooding through me.

"That's enough," the guard barks, pulling me off to the side. "Your time is up."

My eyes stay locked on Maedic Aran, who gives me a beaming smile before turning to the next in line. My breath catches.

He's not going to say anything? Shouldn't he be outraged? Shouldn't he be disgusted?

I stumble a few steps out of the way, not accustomed to the full use of my limbs. I bend my back this way and that, reveling in the freedom of movement. Tears flow when I softly touch my face, and I don't wince in pain. I cry harder when the salty liquid doesn't burn my skin.

I glance around to see several people watching me. But their eyes hold no repulsion, only understanding.

Barely seeing through my bleary eyes, I face Maedic Aran.

"Thank you!" I manage to utter through my sobs of disbelief, knowing full well the distance between us should prevent my words from reaching him.

Yet still, he glances at me with a soft smile on his lips, assuring me the message was received and understood.

His final nod before turning back to the crowd cascades over me like a blessing. I practically float away, head held high.

For the first time in twenty years, I feel like a person again.

I am perfectly and fully alive!

WHY ME?

Timeless Rose

Being sucked into a magical dimension with my seventy-year-old charge and her pet cat was not on my to-do list. But we've all got days that just don't go according to plan, right?

The morning started innocently enough, with a boring stack of never-ending paperwork lasting me well into the afternoon. I drove to an appointment at 3:30, irritable thanks to only having a scrounged lunch that consisted of a granola bar, a half-eaten package of crackers, and disgustingly warm water that had been sitting in my car since the last grocery run ... about two weeks ago.

I finally parked in front of a small, idyllic cottage with a sprawling green lawn surrounded by a white picket fence. Grabbing my new-patient folder from the backseat, I followed the gravel walk to the freshly-painted teal front door, admiring the window boxes full of bright, blooming tulips.

The door swung open to reveal a petite woman in faded jeans and a periwinkle shirt. My gaze dropped to her feet. No shoes or socks. The corners of my mouth quivered when her tiny, caramel-colored toes gave a little wiggle. Jerking my eyes back to her face, I saw her frowning at the HOME HELP HERE! logo emblazoned underneath ALEXIS on my red shirt.

Used to this reaction, I plastered on my professional smile and held out my hand, belatedly realizing her left was holding onto the doorknob, and her right was filled with cream-colored yarn and two long, thick knitting needles.

"Hello," I said in a too-chipper voice. "You must be Mrs. Rose Berk. I'm—"

"I know who you are," Rose sniffed. "You're the babysitter my children and grandchildren are trying to force on me, citing their 'deep concern' about my health. But in reality, you're just their spy." She brandished her knitting needles at me, emphasizing her last words.

First meetings in my business weren't always pleasant, but I was at a loss with this one. My patients weren't typically this ... energetic.

"I—I'm a home health aide." Don't ask me why that was the only thing my brain could come up with to say. I blame low blood sugar.

Rose snorted.

Of course, my stomach chose that moment to make the loudest rumble in the history of rumbles. My cheeks flushed.

Rose's glare, on the other hand, softened. I think she almost smiled at me. After an eternal moment of embarrassment, she stepped aside.

"Come in," she said with a sigh. "I can't send a hungry child off without feeding them."

I wanted to say that at twenty-five, I wasn't exactly a child, but my stomach cramping in hunger kept my mouth shut. I followed her to a bright kitchen with rose motifs covering the walls, and a glass door that opened into a beautifully-groomed backyard. Beyond the manicured lawn and blooming flower plots loomed thick woods that gave off a gloomy air compared to the bright cottage.

Rose busied herself preparing something that smelled like it was seasoned with more than salt and pepper. When my mouth began to water, I decided expanding my culinary skills to more than take-out and boxed mac 'n' cheese was urgent.

Partly to distract myself from the food, I snuck a glance at my patient files again. I had been led to believe my newest charge was frail and suffering from dementia-like symptoms. I narrowed my eyes at the robust woman who was not only surprisingly muscular for a senior citizen, but was almost bouncing from fridge to pantry to stove to counter. Why was I here?

Meow! A grey cat jumped onto my papers, surprising a muffled squeal out of me.

"Misty, you know you're not supposed to be on the table," Rose gently scolded.

She scooped the cat up with one hand and presented a tantalizing plate of yellow rice, red chicken, and something round and fried. I thought rice was white? Whatever. It all looked delicious.

"Thank you!" I was about to dig in when movement in the garden caught my eye.

Looking out the glass door, I did a double take.

"Isn't it a little early for roses to be blooming?" I squinted. "Were those there before?"

"Of course, they were," Rose said quickly, stepping in front of the door.

I warred with my curiosity and hunger for a few seconds, then decided all questions could be answered after food. But I only had time for one delectable mouthful before there was a rapid knock on the door Rose was trying to block from my view.

She gave a disgruntled sigh.

"Yes, Ryder. Hello," Rose greeted the tall young man with green-tinted skin who stepped into the kitchen.

I had never, ever heard of a medical condition that turned a whole body that color. Surprisingly, he wasn't grotesque. He almost looked like polished jade.

"Timeless Rose! You are needed again. It's a new—" Ryder caught sight of me. "Who is she?"

To everyone's surprise, Misty jumped from Rose's arms to curl up and purr on my lap.

Rose studied Misty a moment before saying, "It's complicated."

"This is urgent, Rose." Ryder lowered his voice, but I could still hear. "We don't have time to do anything with her. She'll have to come with us."

Again, I blame lack of food for the fact that my brain didn't react to their whispered words and only focused on Ryder. While I stared in fascination at his waist-length, snow-white hair, Rose had gone and reappeared with well-worn hiking boots and a black leather trench coat in her arms. Now distracted by that odd combination, I watched her stuff knitting needles and yarn into a large pocket, then finally look at me.

"Come on, we've no time to lose," Rose ordered. "You can carry Misty. She's taken an unusual shine to you."

"I should probably go ... try to wake up now." I stood up mechanically, causing Misty to cry in protest as she dropped to the floor.

"Oh, this is better than a dream." Rose smiled for the first time.

Somehow, the glint of excitement in her eyes made me shiver.

Ryder picked up Misty, then he and Rose each grabbed an arm and dragged me toward a six-foot-tall rose bush. How had I missed that earlier?

When vine-like tendrils reached out to us and started twining around our legs, my brain finally started working. Sort of.

"Wait!" I cried, trying to turn back toward the kitchen. "My food!"

I

For more information about Timeless Rose, go to ErudessaGentian.com/writing

MONSTERS MADE

FAIRYTALE RETELLING OF GEORGE AND THE DRAGON

A man and his horse crested a mountain, looking far down on a valley. The man was a warrior named George, who had just been given his first holiday in three years. Three long years of fighting wars, battling monsters, and cheating death. He enjoyed his work, but was looking forward to some relaxation.

He rode atop a magnificent black stallion named Arthur, his trusty companion through thick and thin. George had curly brown hair, with blue eyes set in a handsome face often sighed over by any lady who saw it. But at this moment, his head and muscular body were covered in a full suit of armor; usually shiny, but now dulled somewhat by a thin covering of dust from several days' ride through the countryside.

As George and Arthur peered down into the valley, a delightful view met their gaze. A large sparkling lake took place of honor, surrounded by dark trees and shrubs. Rolling green hills behind the lake were dotted with structures, giving hope of a village nearby.

"Isn't that a sight for sore eyes!" George sighed. "Come, Arthur, this seems a good place to have lunch."

Arthur, also eager for a long, cool drink, started downhill at a happy trot. But as they neared the lake, a putrid stench filled the unnaturally quiet air. There was no songbird to lift the spirits, no rustling of leaves in a refreshing breeze. In fact, the reason the trees looked dark from a distance was because they were burnt black. What George had mistaken as brush were actually scorched patches of earth.

Perhaps this wasn't the oasis it first appeared to be.

George silently drew his sword, alert for any sign of imminent danger. Arthur slowed his steps, carefully avoiding the crunch of ashes beneath his hooves.

They were about to leave this foul place behind altogether, when the fluttering movement of white fabric across the lake caught their attention.

Was that a human? Urging Arthur forward, George still kept a watchful eye all around, in case of ambush.

As they approached, the white fabric became a beautiful dress covering an even more beautiful young damsel. A young, beautiful damsel in distress, they soon realized. She was tied to the charred remains of a tree.

"What happened?" George called out as Arthur brought them next to the beautiful, crying woman.

She turned her beautiful but sorrowful face to him. Wavy blonde hair blew into dark eyes that George was sure would normally be considered bewitching, but were currently swollen and tinged red from crying.

"Please leave, good sir! Save yourself." She sobbed.

"Why are you here?" George asked, dismounting and coming over to cut her bonds.

"No!" She shook her head when she saw what he meant to do. "You must leave! The dragon will destroy everything it sees."

"Dragon?" George immediately stood in front of the woman, sword at the ready to defend her life.

Even Arthur snorted and stamped his hoof, remaining loyally by George's side.

When no mighty, fire-breathing beast appeared, George went back to freeing the distressed damsel.

But when she was finally free, she surprised George by refusing to leave for safety.

"I cannot go."

"Why not?" George asked, exasperated.

The woman sat primly down beside the lake.

Deciding there was no immediate danger, Arthur went to get a drink, and George took off the metal coverings. He preferred his leather armor anyway, for ease of movement.

He then settled in next to the woman to hear her story. Her voice started out small and tight, but as she continued, it grew stronger.

"My name is Elaine." She inclined her head in a slight bow. "I thank you for attempting to save me from my fate. But for the good of my people, I cannot escape it. My father is the leader of the town over yonder." Elaine pointed toward the hills George had spotted some structures on earlier. "We have been plagued by a horrible nightmare."

Elaine shuddered for a moment, but soon continued.

"When the dragon first came, it contented itself with the occasional raid on our farms. But it soon began to bring more and more destruction. We finally began giving it an offering of a single sheep once a week here, at the lake, in an attempt to curb its raids. And it worked. Unfortunately, we soon ran out of sheep. After that, the cattle were sacrificed. Then the swine, then the poultry. But when all the supply of livestock and pets ran dry, we didn't know what to do."

George wanted to say something, but he decided to finish the story before passing judgment.

"The dragon started attacking the village again, but the only thing we had left alive in the village was us," Elaine said sadly.

George stiffened. "Tell me you aren't here as a morsel for the dragon?" He demanded angrily.

"There is no other way to appease it!" Elaine cried helplessly. "My father ruled the offering would be drawn by lots. Everyone in the village had to be in it, so it could be completely fair."

"Fair?" George sputtered.

Elaine went on, as if she didn't notice his outburst. "My name was finally drawn. If I can keep my people safe for another week, I will happily make that sacrifice."

George stood up, horrified.

"Why did you not send for help?" he demanded.

"We tried once we ran out of animals!" Elaine blinked tear-filled eyes at him. "But the messengers never returned, no one ever appeared to fight the dragon, and our attempts ended only in our loss."

"I cannot let this senselessness continue." George was incensed. "Do you have any idea—"

Before he could go any farther, a roar split the air. Elaine lost all color in her face and began to tremble.

"Can you swim?" George scanned the skies, plans forming in his head. "We don't have time to get you to safety."

Elaine shook her head. No sign of the dragon yet, but there was also no shelter anywhere near them. George's gaze landed on Arthur, stamping his hoof impatiently.

George pulled Elaine to her feet. "I have an idea."

⁂

Elaine waited by the lake's edge on Arthur, shivering with fear. A dark dot appeared on the horizon. Elaine trembled, but resisted squeezing the horse with her legs as she watched her fate fly closer and closer.

A brown dragon began to dive right for her, but aborted his course when two successive arrows bounded off his nose and under his eye, while a third sank into his ear.

Roaring in surprise and pain, the dragon flew to the far side of the lake, attempting to dislodge the arrow stuck in his sensitive ear.

George emerged from the lake, water pouring out of the hinges in his armor. Now he remembered why this wasn't a good idea. As the extra weight slowly dripped away, George loosed another volley of arrows before running toward the dragon.

"Go now!" he yelled to Elaine and Arthur.

Elaine clung to his mane as Arthur exploded up the nearest hill.

George kept the dragon's attention away from the escaping duo. Two of his arrows had pierced a leathery wing, but the others merely bounced off the brown scales. It was a small dragon, about the size of ten horses. It couldn't be more than ten years old. George hoped that meant it wouldn't be too battle savvy.

Throwing aside his bow, George drew his sword as he came up on the now angry dragon. He jumped to stay out of a putrid stream of fire. The dragon tried to escape by flying, but the holes made by arrows threw off his balance, and he ended up crashing near where George was taking shelter behind a burnt tree.

Since this was a relatively small beast, George tried to scramble up the foreleg. But he forgot young dragon scales were so slippery! As they grew older, the scales became more abrasive and possible to climb.

George fell with a thud, right next to a razor sharp claw as long as his arm. He narrowly avoided the dragon's foot slamming down in an attempt to crush him.

Putting his sword back in it's sheath, George ran as fast as he could, jumping on the dragon's tail. Using the raised humps that ran all the way down the spine and tail, George made his way toward the dragon's neck. No easy task, as the dragon lashed his tail in an attempt to shake the knight off. When that didn't work, he stamped his feet in frustration. When George slipped a bit, the dragon began bucking and running in circles, throwing the occasional jet of flame into the air.

Finally reaching the dragon's neck, George drew his sword and plunged it into the dragon's weak spot, at the bottom of the skull.

The dragon shuddered, letting out a pitiful wail, before slumping to the ground.

George retrieved his sword, then slid down the foreleg; on purpose, this time.

Landing next to the dying dragon's head, he looked into the dark eye. There, he saw confusion. Of course. Anger and pity warred in George's chest.

"I'm so sorry," he whispered, as the fire of life slowly extinguished inside the dragon.

Hearing hoofbeats behind him, George turned to see Arthur and Elaine coming toward him.

"Give me just a little time, my lady, and I will take you home."

George, Elaine, and Arthur, dragging the dragon's head behind him, entered what felt like an abandoned village. There was a heavy silence that hung over everything.

Elaine directed them toward her father's house. As Arthur clip-clopped past the shuttered houses, people finally began to peek out windows and doors. They had a large, astonished following by the time Elaine said they were at their destination.

Her father came running out the front door. "Elaine? Is that really you?"

He gathered her in his arms as they shared joyful tears.

"This is Sir George," Elaine eventually wiped away her tears to introduce George. "He is the brave knight who saved my life. All our lives. The dragon is slain!"

George had a stony look on his face as the dragon's head was surrounded by the cheering townspeople.

"To our hero!" They cried.

"Enough!" George's voice boomed, stilling everyone's celebrations. "I do not want your cheers, or thanks. Do you not understand?" The anger in his voice made everyone near him flinch. "All of this death was completely unnecessary!"

"What do you mean, unnecessary?" Elaine's father glowered at George. "None of us were able to take on this beast."

"You should have sent for help as soon as the dragon showed up!" George roared. "You have no idea what you did, do you?" He glared right back.

Elaine's father looked embarrassed. The townspeople started murmuring amongst themselves. But George's next words shut everybody up.

"The dragon would have left within a week, if you hadn't started giving it regular, free meals. You practically *trained* the dragon to expect it!"

Elaine looked sick. Her father turned pale. The townsfolk began whispering again.

George turned to them. "You might want to think about some new leadership. I brought the head as proof of the dragon's death. But I hope you also take it as a reminder and warning. Your very own actions can create the monster you fear."

George remounted Arthur, and left the town to their fate.

WHAT'S IN A GIFT?

K ai Zimer had an amazingly useless gift. His singing voice had been praised as "angelic" and "magical." But what use did Merfolk have for a male Siren?

Musical surface jobs were only open to mermaids. They were the ones who seduced human males to learn about their cultures and technology. It was from the reports and loot of these Sirens that Merfolk inventors made similar items for Merkind.

While there were proposals to open up some Siren roles to males due to the rise in human female sailors, it hadn't happened yet. The two most popular career choices for mermen were tending the coral farms or joining the military. But since he couldn't even keep a shellplant alive for more than a week, he would never make it as a farmer. And his jellyfish-like physical coordination rendered the classic trident more of a threat to himself than his adversary.

Of course, there were entertainment arts like theatre. With his combination of nearly coal-black scales, pale skin, aquamarine hair, emerald-green eyes, and abundance of musical talent, he had a fair chance of being successful there. He didn't *hate* his voice, exactly.

In fact, he loved music. He just wished it wasn't his *only* talent. Because what good would being a star, or having any regular office job for that matter, do for Merkind?

After another long day of fruitless job hunting, Kai's shoulders drooped and his tail felt heavy as he swam toward home. Even the brightly colored coral and shell homes in his neighborhood failed to cheer him up. Forget about making a difference for aquatic kind. He couldn't even obtain ordinary, boring employment.

Attempting to shake his sulky mood, Kai tried to focus on his surroundings. But instead of elevating his grim outlook on life, he became aware of the unease that had become part of daily life over the last few months. An undercurrent of turbulence and danger spreading far across the oceans.

Deciding to comfort himself with a treat, Kai swam to the quaint little shop near his home, Berty's Barnacle Bakery. The building was made of dark barnacles, covered with white and green spots. Their outdoor seating had polished coral tables and comfortable clam seats decorated to match the bakery walls. The delicious smells that wafted in the water around the building always wrapped him in a feeling of comfort.

Berty's clever use of volcanic vents gave their baked goods an edge that hot stone bakeries just couldn't match. Not to mention, their flavored bubbles were sublime.

Kai joined the long line waiting to order and looked over the daily specials menu.

In the midst of an internal debate about adding a barnacle brownie to his order of algae espresso bubbles, he heard a soft voice.

"Shark attack reports have been pouring in lately, some claiming to be dangerously close to the city borders."

Glancing to his left, Kai saw two mermaids sitting near the open-shuttered window. One had short pink hair, dark chocolate skin, and emerald scales. Her friend had sand-colored skin with a golden tinge that suggested she was a siren. They were usually the only ones who stayed on the surface long enough to get a tan. She had fiery red hair pulled back in a loose braid and sapphire-blue scales.

"I've even heard about some dolphin attacks!" The pink-haired mermaid said nervously before taking a bite from her muffin.

Her friend nodded solemnly. "My surface shift starts in two days, but I'm getting worried about the trip. If dolphins are being aggressive toward us, then the Saint still isn't in control of her powers."

"I haven't heard anything about coral farms being affected yet. But if she doesn't get it together soon, we won't be the only ones in danger."

The line shuffled forward, and Kai couldn't eavesdrop anymore. But he mulled over what he heard even after arriving at his purple shellhouse.

There must be something wrong with the Saint's magic.

The Mermaid Saint was one born with the Magic of the Ocean. Without their control, chaos would overturn peace, death would devour life. Their magic kept the water's predators from going on a killing spree, underwater volcanoes and vortexes from obliterating half the ocean floor, and the coral reefs vibrant.

When a new Saint came into power, there was always a short period of fluctuation as they got used to their role. But that usually lasted a couple months, at the most. The newest Saint had entered the palace over half a year ago, and danger through the oceans grew every day.

Kai sighed. Now *that* was a gift. To protect all of water life *was* a huge responsibility, but what he wouldn't give to be *useful*.

He whiled the time away with busywork, attempting to keep his growing anxiety at bay. Failing at that, he finally decided to head back out.

Night had long since fallen, but strategically-placed bioluminescent algae gave a gentle glow that normally felt warm and inviting. Tonight, however, the dark waters that lurked just beyond the light appeared more sinister than normal. Kai shivered as he remembered the disturbing reports he had been hearing all day. He swam a little faster, trying not to flinch at every crab that scuttled in and out of the shadows.

Almost unconsciously, Kai ended up at a small seagrass park near the palace grounds that his parents used to take him to as a child.

The happiest moments of his life had all happened here. It's where he forced his parents to listen to the first song he wrote, where they enjoyed their kelp sandwich picnics, and where his father attempted to teach him wrestling.

Kai made his way to the small sandpit in the corner. Someone had built up a pile against a large rock. Smiling to himself, he settled down on the sand, leaning his back against the rock. Gently swishing his tail in front of him, he played with the schools of tiny fish that came up to investigate him.

He let his eyes wander, admiring the towering palace across the sandy road. Lights shone through the occasional window. Oceana's flag, a lobster-red trident on a seaweed-green field, waved strong and proud atop shining white walls that practically glowed, even at night.

Enjoying the soft current swirling through the park like his memories, Kai took a deep breath of water, opened his mouth, and launched into song.

<hr>

The next morning, Kai woke from a dead sleep to loud trumpet fanfare.

"What? What's going on?" He flopped out of his giant plumose anemone bed, still half asleep.

He hadn't spent long in the park singing, but it was still pretty late by the time he made it home.

"A proclamation from the palace!" A tinny voice projected through the water. "All mermen singers are called to the palace by royal decree. All mermen singers are called—"

The voice repeated the proclamation several times before ending the announcement.

Kai couldn't imagine what the palace needed male singers for, but he quickly swam through his shellhouse to brush his teeth with soft coral and search for a clean shirt. Why in oceana hadn't he done laundry last night? He finally found a green one that matched his eyes and wasn't too wrinkly.

On his way to the palace, Kai began to wonder if something was different in the water. Did the city seem a little brighter than usual? The atmosphere lighter, calmer? Even he felt like smiling and laughing, which hadn't been the norm for a while.

When Kai got to the palace, he joined the long line already formed in front of the door. Eventually reaching the front, he gave his name, answered a few personal questions from a young mermaid who carefully wrote everything down, then was herded into a side yard to wait.

He soon joined a group of ten mermen as they were led into the palace.

Kai's group followed their guide into a plain room full of chairs. Again left to wait, they chatted amiably among themselves. One by one, they were summoned, the room emptying without anyone returning.

When Kai was finally called, he silently swam behind a muscle-bound palace guard into a grand hall.

He gazed at a set of splendid thrones made from the purest white coral for a moment before realizing where he was floating. He was called before the very King and Queen themselves? There they were, regal and completely intimidating.

The throne room looked more like a hall. Gold decorations adorned the cream walls. The high ceiling was painted with a colorful array of ocean flora. Ruby-red curtains covered tall windows, casting a rosy glow about the room.

Behind the thrones, a large version of the kingdom's flag was stretched out.

Sitting tall, the Queen's soft pink tail was gracefully draped over her throne's edge. A thin gold crown sat atop her pink and white hair. With soft grey eyes and the hint of a smile, she gave off a gentle atmosphere. The King's posture wasn't quite as rigid, and his thick gold tail gave a small thrash that whistled through the water before relaxing. Black, curly hair rested under a matching gold crown and framed a handsome face that was somewhat soured by a very stern expression. Perhaps he was just tired from a long day of interviews.

Finally coming to his senses, Kai gave a deep bow.

"Kai Zimer?" the Queen's melodic voice asked.

"Yes, Your Majesty," Kai answered, still in a deep bow.

"Do you know any lullabies?" The King didn't speak loudly, but his voice still managed to ring through the whole hall, imperious and strong.

"I do, Your Majesty," Kai said, looking up in puzzlement.

"Any one will do." The Queen nodded. "You may begin."

Still confused, Kai started singing the first song that came to mind, the one that ended his impromptu performance for the fish and clams last night.

It had been a favorite of his mother's, and almost never failed to lift his spirits.

Before he'd finished the first verse, there was a noticeable waver in the water. A relaxing, happy feeling permeated the hall. A corner of the banner behind the thrones was pulled back, and a hooded figure swam forward.

Power radiated from this stranger, causing Kai to involuntarily back up. As if an unexpected performance for royalty hadn't made him nervous enough.

"It's him!" The hooded figure pointed to Kai.

The power in the feminine voice made little waves throughout the hall.

"What did I do?" he asked, not sure whether to be anxious or confused.

Both seemed like a good plan for now.

"Your voice is the miracle we've been looking for!" the King said, his stern expression relaxing into a beaming smile.

"We searched for you half the night." The relief in the Queen's voice somehow made Kai feel guilty.

Before he could ask any questions, the figure in front of him threw back her hood.

"I am the Mermaid Saint," she said.

Kai tried not to gawk at her. The Saint was glowing! Her rainbow-colored hair sparkled. Tiny, glowing blue runeish designs decorated the exposed skin of her face and throat. The solid cream-colored shirt had long sleeves with material so thin, you could just make out more of those blue runes on her arms. Her kelp-green eyes looked a little haunted, but grew more peaceful by the second. Kai could still feel the magic emanating from her, though it was softer than before.

"My power has remained unstable," the Saint told him. "Until I heard your songs last night."

"My songs?" Kai could hardly believe what he was hearing.

The Saint nodded. "Your voice, it would seem, calms my power. As soon as I realized this, scouts were sent to find you. But your singing stopped before we could pinpoint your location."

Kai almost apologized before remembering it wasn't against the law to stop singing and go to sleep when you were tired.

"Will you stay in the palace and help me?" the Saint asked. "There is much damage I need to right."

It took a moment for Kai to snap out of his shock. Was it really possible *he* could be of use to the Mermaid Saint—protector of all Ocean life? This was more than he could have ever dreamed. Somehow, he managed to nod his head.

"T-thank you!" he said, still overwhelmed.

The next bit was a blur. He barely remembered being dismissed by the King and Queen, or following the Saint along a glittering hallway as she explained what his new life was going to look like. He was pretty sure she said something about sharks, and dangerous trenches—and maybe a tsunami?—before he got completely distracted with the heavenly music room he now had complete access to.

Over the following weeks, as Kai and the Saint learned how to work together, a thought occurred to him.

Kai Zimer had an amazingly useful gift after all.

The original flash version of What's in a Gift can be found at GoHavok.com

CRASHED PLANS

“ **A** re you too wired to get some rest, Will?”
Jessica’s question jolted Williric out of his thoughts.

“I guess so.” Will smiled. “I’ll probably regret not taking a nap later.”

“Probably.” Jessica grinned back. “We’ve still got a couple hours to go. We’re … somewhere over the Amazon jungle.” Jessica peered out the airplane window, as if she would be able to recognize landmarks from over 30,000 feet in the air. “Well, if you’re not going to rest, let’s go over what we know again.”

Will’s heart swelled with warmth as his one and only cousin reached for the old leather bag under the seat in front of her. Jessica’s enthusiasm for a good mystery helped him continue the search for his origins, no matter how many dead-ends they encountered.

“I’ve been going over it in my head anyway, so I might as well say it out loud,” Will agreed.

“All right,” Jessica said, deepening her voice for dramatic effect. “Let’s start with when Uncle Brock found you in the jungles of the Amazon.”

“Right. Dad took a tour in South America when a wounded man stumbled out of the jungle. He was holding me and carrying this leather bag. Before dying, he put the two stones around my neck."

Will and Jessica pulled their nearly identical necklaces out to compare. According to the story, they used to be ruby red, with an emerald center. When Will first found them in the bag, they were black. After he touched them, they turned emerald. The stone he gifted Jessica also changed. The green faded to the middle of the stone while the edges faded back to the original black.

"When we were younger, I thought these were mood rocks." Jessica chuckled. "But they just turn the one color, no matter who touches them."

Will nodded, again baffled by these strange stones. They were about a thumb's length, thin, smooth, and oblong. The emerald color glowed softly, but that was only noticeable when you were in a dark space.

"The single word uttered by the stranger before his final breath was *Williric*." Jessica breathed his name like she was dying. "Which is why uncle Brock decided to make that your official name."

Will rolled his eyes. Sometimes having a professional actress as your cousin added so much drama.

The question of his origins had always stayed tucked away in the back of his mind; but after the death of his adopted parents, it changed from a slight tickle into a growing need to know.

Ever-curious, Jessica had found a hidden compartment in the old leather bag that held a small notebook. The cousins spent the last two years attempting to decipher the codes and diagrams found there. Now, they were on their way to Peru, retracing Brock's original trip.

Will opened the notebook to the drawing of an island. Or, what they guessed was an island. This page they studied the most. No matches could be found on any maps they looked at. But then again, most of the Amazon remained uncharted.

Will tapped the image. "The stranger must have come from this island. We find the island, we find some answers."

Maybe where I came from, he added to himself.

"I still think it could be the drawing of a territory, not necessarily an island," Jessica mused, taking the notebook from Will.

"There's a cove, right there." Will pointed.

"Sure. So, at least part of this area touches water. That doesn't mean all of it does." Jessica shook her head.

As they started bickering about this old point again, a bad spot of turbulence ended their argument. Will glanced at their fellow passengers. Most were watching a movie or reading something. A few were trying to sleep.

"Will?" Jessica pointed out her window. "Have you ever seen something like this?"

Will peered at a thick, green fog surrounding their plane.

"Is that lightning?" Worry edged her question as they saw bright crackling in the strange fog.

"Maybe I should put this away." Will returned the notebook into their waterproof bag.

Before he could settle it back under his seat, the plane gave a terrific shudder, then took a sharp dive.

Screams filled the air as everyone realized what was happening.

"Will!" Jessica clutched his hand on top of their shared armrest.

Seconds stretched into stomach-churning moments of terror, tears, and regrets before the plane leveled off.

The wailing subsided as their speed slowed.

"Are we ok?" Jessica asked through clenched teeth.

Will dared to peek out the window, only to watch them crash into turbulent waves that ripped the plane in two.

Will groaned as he struggled to sit up straight. Icy water rushed into what remained of the plane.

"You okay?" Will's voice slurred as he struggled to bring his cousin into focus.

Jessica was slumped over, blood trickling down her face.

"Jess! Jessica, wake up!" Will scrambled to unbuckle their seat belts.

He worked with blinding speed to throw their life jackets on while the plane sank faster. The water lapped at their necks when Will secured his bag and struggled them both out of the wreck and to the surface.

Will couldn't see or hear anything over the raging storm. Not even his own screams for help. He pulled the still unresponsive Jessica close, trying to shield her from the rough waves.

It seemed an eternity to Will, floating in the cold storm, before he caught sight of something to their right during a flash of lightning.

Williric attached their life vests together using his belt, then started swimming.

⚜

Warm sunlight greeted Will as he opened tired eyes.

"Ouch!" he groaned, body stiff from sleeping on a stone cave floor.

Will glanced around in confusion. How did they get here? He remembered being exhausted and cold from swimming, then his memories blanked.

He took a few steps to the cave entrance and observed the large expanse of water. Ten yards away, the ocean's calm edge now lapped against the sand, instead of last night's thunderous crashing.

Rocks and water hedged his left and a narrow beach with a grassy bluff hugged his right. Though not visible, bird calls joined the ocean's murmuring on the breeze. At least they weren't the only life here. Wherever here was.

"Will?" Jessica's sleepy voice cut through his musings.

"Jess?" Will ran to her side. "Are you all right?"

"I think so. My head just hurts a bit." Jessica gingerly touched the cut that still had little bits of dried blood.

"It doesn't look too bad." Will inspected it closer. "But it's been a few years since I brushed up on my first aid," he quipped.

"Where are we?" Jessica turned her head to observe the darker surrounding of the cave.

The narrow stone enclosure wasn't inviting, but it was dry. The walls yawned into pitch blackness, suggesting deeper caverns.

"I don't know," Will said. "My GPS was in my suitcase."

"Hey, you managed to save the bag." Jessica peered in. "And it looks like the notebook survived!" She held it up triumphantly.

"It can't help us much at the moment," Will reminded her. "We should search for any other survivors and try to figure out where we are."

"Agreed." Jessica sobered.

After scouring the nearby beach proved fruitless, they decided turning their attention to the problem of provisions was prudent.

"I'll search the cave," Will volunteered. "There might be some fresh water further back."

"And I'll see if there's anything edible on the bluff."

After making sure Jessica found decent foot- and handholds to climb, Will headed back to the cave. He rummaged through his bag until he pulled a small penlight out. The narrow beam flickered but still miraculously worked.

Just beyond the sunlit entrance, Will discovered a small river. He smiled as the clean liquid refreshed his parched throat. At least they had water. He sent the beam of light in a wide arc, revealing a small path beyond the river.

"Will!" Jessica came streaking into the cave.

Not seeing his crouching form, she crashed into him, sending them both flying. Jessica scrambled to her feet, dragging Will further into the darkness.

"I'm sorry," she whispered. "But someone is coming after me!"

"What?" Will followed, the dropped penlight forgotten.

"Some strange guy in brown leather armor-type-stuff surprised me when I was checking out a grove of nearby trees. He saw my necklace, then pointed some long stick at me. He had a sword, and maybe a gun, so I got scared and ran here." Jessica rushed her story as they stumbled along the pitch-black corridor.

"Maybe he could have helped us!" Will nearly turned back.

"I'm sorry, I panicked!" Jessica lamented.

"No, I probably would've done the same, had a stick-wielding, sword-carrying, maybe gun-toting stranger appeared in front of me," Will said, half teasing.

Jessica huffed into the inky blackness. They took a step forward, and the wall they had been feeling their way along disappeared.

"Careful," Jessica called. "I think we might have entered a large chamber."

She felt her way forward, inching away from Will.

"Jess? Don't get too far away from me."

"Shh! I think I heard someone coming down the passage behind us!"

Will pressed himself against the smooth stone. He held his breath but heard nothing.

"Where are you?" he cautiously called. "We should stay together. Oh, there you are. I see you."

They widened their eyes at each other.

"Wait, how can you see me?" Jessica waved her hand. "A minute ago, we couldn't see anything. Now, there's a greenish tint to the air." She squinted at him. "It's coming from behind you!"

Will glanced at the wall. Emerald light emanated from where he touched.

"What in the world?" He leapt away.

There was enough light to make out a stone staircase leading to a ledge about six meters high.

Jessica passed Will to the glowing walls as he made his way toward the stairs.

A tall, muscular man carrying a long stick entered the cave. He wasn't brandishing his sword, but that didn't make him look any less dangerous. He gaped around the room, astonished eyes landing on the emerald stone around Will's neck.

"Jess, be careful!" Will scrambled up the steps, motioning for Jessica to join him.

She hesitated, since the stranger was now closer to the ledge than she was. She started edging her way along the wall, past the riveted stranger.

Will searched for anything to defend themselves with. Catching sight of an old suit of armor, Will grabbed the first thing he could lay his hands on: a sword. Not stopping to think about the fact that he had no weapons training whatsoever, Will charged down the steps, sword held in front of him.

"Who are you?" Will demanded of the still dumbstruck stranger.

"Will, the sword is glowing!" Jessica pointed, wide-eyed.

Giving a small, embarrassing shriek, he threw the sword away and jerked back. Unfortunately, he was reminded how slippery the steps were when he tripped and fell right over the edge.

"Will!" Jessica screamed.

The last thing Williric remembered before blacking out was the stranger leaping forward and crying out, "Your Highness!"

⁂

"Are you sure he'll be all right?" Jessica asked for the tenth time. She paced back and forth. They had come out into the bright sunshine to treat Will's wound.

"Quite sure," their pursuer-turned-protector, patiently restated.

"It's just a little bump on the head," Will reassured Jessica. "I'm fine, now, thanks to ... Selwyn, was it?"

"I was merely doing my job, my Prince." Selwyn bowed.

Jessica bit back a laugh as Will gawked. "Excuse me? Sorry, but I think you have us confused with ... someone else."

Selwyn squinted at Will. "I do not think that is possible. Your name is Williric, is it not? The stone around your neck ... and the cave ... You don't know anything?"

The cousins studied him with confusion. Will reflexively grabbed his necklace.

"Wait, how did you know his full name was Williric?" Jessica asked.

Instead of answering her, Selwyn posed a question. "Who raised you?"

"My parents," Will said shortly.

"Where did you get that bag?" Selwyn pointed to the leather sack that managed to survive this whole adventure so far.

"Why do you want to know?"

"May I look at it?"

Will reluctantly handed it over. Selwyn's fingers traced the faded crest worked into the top flap.

"If you don't know, then that means ... " Selwyn's eyes filled with tears before he blinked them away. "You know nothing of your origins?"

Will perked up. "You know something about my past?"

"Um, guys?" Jessica pointed toward the nearby beach.

Two dozen well-armed men poured out of small boats onto the sand.

Selwyn grabbed Will and Jessica in a panic. "We have to go. There is much you need to know, Your Highness, but for now, hide the stones. Both of you!"

Selwyn stuffed Will's necklace under his shirt, then started dragging them both toward the nearby forest.

"Would you stop calling me that?" Will snapped. "I'm no prince. I wouldn't even know how to act like royalty."

"One does not *act* royal." Selwyn frowned.

"Guys, not the time!" Jessica glanced back at their pursuers.

"You're right." Selwyn shook off everything but his responsibility. "Once you're safe, I can tell you everything."

The three figures disappeared into the trees.

ABOUT THE AUTHOR

ERUDESSA GENTIAN

Erudessa Gentian is a firm believer that clean entertainment can be powerful. Inspired by her love of cultures and learning, she produces dynamic art to spark imagination and touch souls.

Erudessa writes in multiple genres, but specializes in fantasy and science fiction. She posts about lifestyle, travel and so much more on her blog at www.ErudessaGentian.com

For a list of all her stories and upcoming adventures, including her debut science-fantasy series Kynaston Royal Saga, go to www.ErudessaGentian.com/Writing

www.ingramcontent.com/pod-product-compliance
Lightning Source LLC
Chambersburg PA
CBHW032024180726
48283CB00008B/2812